Bat Attack!

After making a few turns in the Mirror Maze, Freddie realized he was lost. He kept on going. Soon he was even more confused.

He soon found himself in a long, empty hallway. After the glaring lights of the maze, it seemed very dim and gloomy.

Freddie started down the hall. Then he heard a funny noise behind him—it was a high-pitched squeak. Freddie looked over his shoulder and froze.

A gigantic purple bat with glowing green eyes was flying down the hallway.

It was heading straight at him!

Books in The New Bobbsey Twins series

Available from MINSTREL Books

THE NEW
Bobbsey
Twins™
#17
THE CASE AT CREEPY CASTLE

LAURA LEE HOPE
ILLUSTRATED BY PAUL JENNIS

A MINSTREL® BOOK

PUBLISHED BY POCKET BOOKS

New York   London   Toronto   Sydney   Tokyo   Singapore

A MINSTREL PAPERBACK *ORIGINAL*

A Minstrel Book published by
POCKET BOOKS, a division of Simon & Schuster Inc.
1230 Avenue of the Americas, New York, NY 10020

ISBN: 0-671-69289-5

First Minstrel Books printing April 1990

10 9 8 7 6 5 4 3 2 1

The NEW BOBBSEY TWINS is a trademark
of Simon & Schuster Inc.

THE BOBBSEY TWINS, A MINSTREL BOOK and colophon
are registered trademarks of Simon & Schuster Inc.

Printed in the U.S.A.

Contents

THE CASE
AT CREEPY
CASTLE

1

Welcome to Creepy Castle

"There it is!" twelve-year-old Nan Bobbsey cried. She pointed out the car window. "There's Creepy Castle!"

"Where?" her younger brother, Freddie, demanded from the backseat. "I don't see anything."

"I don't either," said blond, blue-eyed Flossie. She was Freddie's twin.

Nan's twin, Bert, pointed to the left. "The castle's up there," he said. "But it's hidden by the trees now."

The Bobbseys were on their way to visit an old family friend, Bruce Farman. Mr. Farman lived in the little New England town of Merlin. He was the owner of Merlin's biggest attraction, Creepy Castle. The spooky fun house had just opened for the summer.

"You can see it now," Mr. Bobbsey said.

The twins stared out the window.

A huge castle built of black stone stood on top of a tall hill. Its many towers with pointed roofs made it look like something from a scary movie.

Bert leaned forward to get a better view. "It's creepy all right," he said. "Why would anybody want to live in a place like that?"

"Well, nobody does live there now," Mrs. Bobbsey said. "The man who built it, many years ago, was an actor named Edward Horvath. He was famous for playing vampires in the movies. He was so good at it that some people thought he really was one."

"That's pretty weird," Freddie said.

"But he wasn't a vampire, really. Right, Mom?" Flossie asked.

Mrs. Bobbsey smiled. "Right. Now you kids quiet down while I read Mr. Farman's directions."

A few minutes later Mr. Bobbsey pulled up to a big white house with green shutters. Mr. Farman was sitting in the swing on the front porch. When he saw the car, he came down the steps to greet the Bobbseys.

"I'm so glad you're here," he said. He shook hands with Mr. and Mrs. Bobbsey. Then he gave each twin a hug. "Come on in and have some lemonade."

The Bobbseys trooped into the house after their friend. While their parents and Mr. Farman talked, the twins took their lemonade outside to the porch.

As they were sipping their drinks, a voice called, "Hi!"

The twins looked up and saw a girl of about eleven walking across the lawn. She had long black hair pulled into a ponytail.

The girl stepped onto the porch. "I'm Melissa Webster. I live next door. Are you the Bobbseys?"

Bert introduced himself and the other twins.

Melissa smiled. "Mr. Farman told me you were coming. He said you've solved lots of mysteries."

Freddie nodded proudly. "We're the best detectives around!"

Nan laughed. "I don't know about that. We've solved a lot of cases, though."

"Neat!" said Melissa. "Will you tell me about some of them?"

"Sure," Bert said.

"We can go to the common tomorrow after

lunch," said Melissa. "That's one of my favorite places."

"What's a common?" asked Flossie.

"It's a park in the center of town," Melissa said. "It has a bandstand and a playground and a little pond. It's really pretty."

"That sounds like fun," Nan said. "We can meet you there. But first I think we're going to Creepy Castle."

Melissa nodded. "I've been there. Did you know that Mr. Farman was Mr. Horvath's lawyer? Mr. Horvath didn't have any relatives, so he left the castle to Mr. Farman in his will."

"Is it fun?" Freddie asked.

"Well, it's a little, you know, strange," said Melissa. "Some of the kids tell stories about it."

"Ghost stories?" Freddie said eagerly.

Instead of answering, Melissa looked at her watch. "Uh-oh," she said. "I'd better get home. Don't forget. We'll meet at the common after lunch tomorrow. I really want to hear about your mysteries."

"And we'd like to hear more about Creepy Castle," Nan replied. "We can swap stories."

Melissa nodded, but she didn't look very happy about the idea of talking about the castle. She dashed across the lawn, back to her own house.

The twins went inside and found the grown-ups in the living room. "I've arranged for you kids to have free passes to the castle while you're here," Mr. Farman told them. "I'll take you up there first thing in the morning. I've also rented bikes so you can get around town on your own."

"That's great," Freddie said.

"We'll have time for breakfast first, won't we?" Flossie asked.

Mr. Farman laughed. "Don't worry, Flossie. You'll have plenty of pancakes before you get to the castle."

The next morning, Mr. and Mrs. Bobbsey drove off to visit the nearby antique shops. Mr. Farman drove the twins to Creepy Castle.

The road to the fun house twisted up the hill from the parking lot. Flossie and Freddie jumped out of the car and ran ahead. They came back with wide eyes.

"There's water all around the castle," Flossie reported.

"That water is called a moat," Mr. Farman said. "Mr. Horvath wanted to keep people away from the castle. He liked his privacy."

"There's a drawbridge, too," said Freddie. "Does it really go up?"

"It sure does," Mr. Farman replied.

"Melissa told us that Mr. Horvath left Creepy Castle to you," said Bert.

Mr. Farman nodded. "That's right. You know, the kids around here—and even some adults—were all a little scared of Mr. Horvath." He chuckled. "I was, too, when I was a kid. His vampire movies were pretty frightening."

"But he was just acting," Nan said.

Mr. Farman shrugged. "Yes . . . but he acted the part a little bit too well. He didn't go into town very often. When he did, he always wore his black cape."

Nan looked up at the huge black walls of the castle. She thought she saw a bat fly out of one of the windows. She shivered, then laughed at herself. It was just a pigeon!

They all headed toward the drawbridge. "There's Cara Lassiter," Mr. Farman said. "She's the tall, red-haired woman. She manages the castle for me. The brown-haired woman she's with is Laurel James. Laurel's in charge of all the wonderful special effects. Come on, I'll introduce you."

The two women seemed to be arguing about something. "I'm sick of you telling me what to do all the time," Laurel was saying.

Both Cara and Laurel turned when Mr.

Farman called to them. Nan noticed that Cara Lassiter's mouth was set in a straight line. Laurel James looked angry.

"Cara, Laurel, meet the Bobbsey twins," Mr. Farman said. "I told you about them the other day."

The castle manager took off her big yellow-framed sunglasses and smiled. "Oh, yes, the detectives," she said. "Welcome to Creepy Castle. Laurel, you'd better be on your toes. These kids might figure out all your tricks."

"Maybe," Laurel said. "But there might not be any more tricks to figure out. If things don't get better around here soon, I'm quitting."

She turned and strode over the drawbridge, toward the entrance.

Cara shook her head. "I'll go talk to her, Mr. Farman."

Cara hurried after the special-effects expert. The two women disappeared into the castle.

Mr. Farman frowned. "I can't afford to lose Laurel. Especially now, when we've just opened. Maybe I should talk to her, too."

He thought for a moment. "Would you kids mind being on your own for a little while?" he asked. "If you stay on the first floor of the castle, you can't get lost."

"We don't mind," Nan said. The other Bobbseys nodded in agreement.

"Thanks. Here are your passes. I'll find you after I talk to Cara and Laurel." Mr. Farman handed each of the twins a card printed with a drawing of the castle. Then he hurried away toward the entrance.

"What are we waiting for?" Freddie demanded. "Let's go find some ghosts!"

They crossed the drawbridge and showed their passes to a person in a gorilla costume at the entrance to the castle. The gorilla snorted and thumped his chest. Then he pointed through the large wooden doors toward a long, gloomy hall.

The twins entered the castle and walked down the hall. Their footsteps echoed loudly against the stone walls. But there were too many footsteps.

The Bobbseys stopped and turned around. The hall was deserted except for them, but they could still hear footsteps.

"It's a tape recording," Bert said with a grin. "We probably stepped on a switch somewhere."

"Uh, wait a minute." Freddie glanced up at the walls. Paintings of men and women in old-fashioned clothes were hanging there. "Are the people in those pictures *watching* us?"

Flossie squealed. "Their eyes moved!" she said. "I saw them!"

Nan nodded. "They must be programmed to do that. Let's see."

She walked along the hall. The eyes in the portraits followed her.

"Hey, neat," said Freddie. "I hope the rest of the place is this good." He studied a sign on the wall. "What next? The Lair of the Dragon or the Magical Mirror Maze?"

"Dragons," Bert said.

"Mirrors," Flossie said at the same time.

"How about mirrors first, then dragons?" Nan suggested.

The twins followed arrows to the Mirror Maze. After a few steps into it, the Bobbseys were completely lost. Bert reached out to take Flossie's hand and touched a mirror instead. Nan walked straight into a sheet of glass and bumped her nose. Freddie followed someone for a minute or two before he realized that the someone was himself.

Flossie skipped ahead of the others, pausing here and there to smile at herself in a mirror and pat her blond curls. Suddenly she stopped. Reflected in the mirrors was someone very tall. He was wearing a long black cloak.

Flossie's heart started to pound. She turned around slowly.

The man was standing right behind her. His face was very white, and his lips were bright red. His glittering eyes looked straight at Flossie, and he gave her an evil smile.

Flossie guessed the truth even before she saw his pointed teeth.

The man was a vampire!

2

The Creature in the Mirror

Flossie screamed. Wherever she looked, she saw that white face and those pointed teeth. She covered her eyes with her hands.

Suddenly someone grabbed her shoulders. She was about to let out another yell when she heard Nan say, "What is it, Floss? What's the matter?"

Flossie slowly uncovered her eyes. The vampire had vanished! "Did you see him?" she demanded. "Where did he go?"

Nan looked puzzled. "Who?" she asked.

Freddie and Bert came up then.

"What's going on?" Bert asked.

"I saw a vampire right there in the mirror," she said, pointing. "A *real* vampire."

"Wow!" Freddie said. "I wish I'd seen him."

"Come on, let's search the maze," Bert suggested. "He can't be far away."

They wandered through the Mirror Maze, but there was no trace of the vampire.

"I did see him," Flossie said. "Really and truly. He was standing right behind me."

Bert patted her shoulder. "Maybe you just saw somebody's face that was distorted by the mirrors."

"It was a vampire," Flossie insisted. "He looked exactly like the ones in the movies."

"I know!" said Freddie. "Maybe it was an actor who works here. You know, made up to *look* like a vampire."

Flossie shivered. "Let's get out of here," she said. "I don't want to see him again."

"Okay," Bert said. "This way—I think."

After a few more minutes in the Mirror Maze, the twins found themselves back in the main hall.

"Now let's try the Lair of the Dragon," said Freddie.

Flossie looked at the dark stone walls. They seemed to be pressing in on her. "I want to go outside," she announced.

"But we've seen only one thing so far," Freddie pointed out.

"We can always come back later," Nan said quickly. "We have our passes, remember?"

"Well, kids," Mr. Farman said from behind them. "How do you like Creepy Castle so far?"

"It's excellent," Freddie said. "We got lost in the Mirror Maze for a while, though."

Mr. Farman laughed. "Even I get lost now and then."

Flossie tugged on his sleeve. "I saw the vampire," she said.

"The vampire?" Mr. Farman repeated.

Flossie nodded. "He had a white face and red lips and pointed teeth."

Mr. Farman frowned. "That's strange," he said.

"What do you mean, Mr. Farman?" Bert asked.

Mr. Farman shook his head slowly. "I know all the actors here. There's one thing I can tell you for sure. We don't have anyone who plays a vampire."

"I don't get it," Freddie said.

Flossie had just finished telling Melissa about her adventure at Creepy Castle that morning. The three of them were sitting on the grass of the common. Nan and Bert had gone to the nearby shops to buy a few things.

"That vampire *had* to be an actor," Freddie continued. "What else could he have been?"

"I don't know," Flossie said. "But I hope I never see him again!"

Melissa didn't say anything. She pulled up a blade of grass and started to chew on it.

"I did see a vampire," Flossie insisted.

"Oh, I believe you," Melissa said. "But—"

"What?" Freddie and Flossie said together.

"Well," Melissa said, "before Creepy Castle opened last summer, kids used to sneak in sometimes. Some of them said they'd seen strange lights and heard weird noises. After that, nobody wanted to go back. Kids started saying that the guy who built the castle was a *real* vampire. They even say that he's still there, in a secret room somewhere."

"I don't believe that," Freddie said. "Do you?"

Melissa was pulling apart another blade of grass. "No," she said. "I guess not. But I still don't think I'd like to spend the night in Creepy Castle."

Bert studied the shopping list. Then he looked at the shelf in the food market again. "All Mr. Farman said was New England baked beans," he said to Nan. "Which brand do you think he wants?"

Nan put a finger to her lips. "Shh," she said. A man and a woman were standing behind Bert, talking about Creepy Castle.

". . . spoils the town," the woman said. She took a can off the shelf and dropped it into her shopping cart. "The place attracts too many tourists."

"You're right," the man said. "Last summer it took me half an hour just to drive through town. The same thing will happen this summer."

"The castle should be closed down," the woman continued. "It could be turned into something else—a school or a museum. We don't need a fun house."

"Well, visitors do spend a lot of money here," the man said. "That's good for the town."

"Hmmph," the woman said as she and the man walked away.

"Boy, what a grouch," Bert said. "I think Creepy Castle is neat."

Nan nodded. "Every town should have a fun house."

The twins finished their shopping. Nan paid at the check-out, and they stepped outside.

"Next, the drugstore," said Bert.

He and Nan walked a few doors down to Phillips's Drugstore. It had an old-fashioned look inside and out. A friendly-looking bald man stood behind the counter. He was wearing a jacket with big bright blue and gray checks.

"I'll be with you two in just a minute," he said. He reached into his pants pocket and pulled out a big gold watch. Then he flipped open the top and looked up at a large clock on the wall.

"Just making sure that old clock is telling the right time," he said. He smiled at Bert and Nan. "Now, what can I do for you?"

"Could I please have a roll of film?" Bert asked.

The man found the film on the shelf behind him. He set the small box on the counter.

"There you are," the man said. "Anything else today, youngsters?"

"No, thank you," Nan said. "Are you Mr. Phillips?"

"Doug Phillips, that's me," he replied.

"I really like your pocket watch," Nan said. "It must be pretty old."

"Oh, it is, young lady," Mr. Phillips replied. "But it keeps perfect time. I always use it." He pulled out the watch again. "It belonged to my

grandfather. He started this drugstore almost a hundred years ago. I've tried to keep it a cozy, friendly place."

"Well, it's really nice," Nan said. She took a ten-dollar bill from her wallet and handed it to Mr. Phillips. To the twins' surprise, the druggist rubbed the bill with his finger. Then he held it up to the light.

"Is something wrong?" Bert asked.

"I'm afraid so," Mr. Phillips said. The smile had vanished from his face. "You're going to have to wait for the police. This bill is counterfeit!"

3

Funny Money

Sergeant Blandsford hung up the telephone in the drugstore. "Okay," he said to Bert and Nan. "Mr. Farman says he knows you."

Bert gave a sigh of relief.

The sergeant held out the ten-dollar bill. "It's fake, all right. Do you kids remember where you got it?"

"At the grocery store," Nan said. "I got back ten dollars in change."

"The grocery store, eh?" Sergeant Blandsford took off his cap and scratched his head. "I'd better go over and talk to the manager. A lot of funny money has been showing up in town during the last week or so."

The sergeant walked to the door. "Goodbye for now, folks."

"What about our film?" Nan asked.

"Don't worry," Mr. Phillips said. "Keep the film."

Nan and Bert thanked Mr. Phillips and left the store. Then they walked across the street to the common.

Freddie and Flossie were still there with Melissa. Nan and Bert told them about their adventure in the drugstore.

"That happened to my friend's mom last week," Melissa said.

"We'd better get back to Mr. Farman's," Bert said. "After that call from Sergeant Blandsford, Mom and Dad might be worrying."

Melissa stood up and brushed the grass off her jeans. "Why don't you guys come swimming this afternoon?" she said. "I'm meeting my friends down at Grover's Lake at four."

"Great," Nan said. "We'll ask Mom and Dad."

Mr. and Mrs. Bobbsey gave their permission. At four o'clock, the twins were pedaling toward Grover's Lake.

When they got to a dirt road, Bert stopped his bike. He looked at the map Mr. Farman had drawn for them. "The lake should be right in the middle of these woods," he said.

"Is it much farther?" asked Flossie. "I'm hot, and my legs are getting tired."

"No, it's— Hey, watch out!" The twins scrambled out of the way just as an old green station wagon came speeding past. The driver was a young woman with short dark hair. She glanced out at them and laughed.

"Boy, some people!" Freddie said in disgust. "Come on, let's find that lake."

After a short ride, the twins came to the lake. Wooden steps led down a grassy hill to a small sandy beach.

"Uh-oh, look who's here," said Freddie. He pointed to the green station wagon parked alongside the road.

"I don't care," Flossie said. She propped her bike against a tree. "The water looks great."

"And there's Melissa and her friends. They're already swimming," Nan added.

Bert let his bike down on the grass. "Last one in is a rotten egg!" he yelled. He pulled off his T-shirt and raced down the steps.

Flossie was right behind him. She pulled off her shorts and T-shirt and tugged at her swimsuit. "Ready or not, here I come!" she called.

She ran down the beach and splashed through the shallow water. Freddie and Bert were already in the lake. Nan was at the other end of the beach, talking to Melissa.

Flossie did a belly flop right next to Freddie.

Freddie clapped his hands together and sent a sheet of water in her direction. Flossie shut her eyes tightly.

"Hey, watch it, you kids!" The angry shout came from just behind Flossie. She opened her eyes and turned around.

A tall young man with a scar on his face was standing a few feet away. He was glaring at her and Freddie. Next to him was the dark-haired woman the twins had seen in the green station wagon.

"You'd better behave yourselves or we'll report you to the lifeguard," the woman said.

The two of them glared at Flossie and Freddie for another moment, then walked away.

"Hi," Melissa said. She and Nan waded over to Flossie. "I'm glad you guys came."

"So am I," Flossie said. "Hey, do you know that man and woman over there?"

Melissa nodded. "Sure," she said. "The guy's name is Rick. He's one of the actors at Creepy Castle. That woman with him is Lily, I think. She works there, too. This must be their afternoon off. Why?"

Flossie shrugged. "Oh, I don't know."

"Want to play tag?" Melissa reached over and tapped Flossie on the shoulder. "You're It!" she cried, and swam off into the lake.

24

"I'll get you!" Flossie shouted, and dived after Melissa.

That evening the telephone rang.

"Excuse me," Mr. Farman said, leaving the dinner table. When he came back a few minutes later, he looked very worried.

"What is it, Bruce?" Mrs. Bobbsey asked.

"I'm not sure," he said. "That was Laurel James. She called to tell me that Cara Lassiter, the manager of the castle, seems to have vanished."

"Oh, come on," Mr. Bobbsey said.

"No, I'm serious," Mr. Farman said. "Cara left the castle this afternoon. A note on her desk said she'd be out for a few minutes. But she never came back at all."

"Maybe she was delayed for some reason," Mrs. Bobbsey said.

"She would have called," Mr. Farman said. "She's a very responsible employee."

"I bet she turned into a vampire," Flossie muttered. Bert kicked her under the table.

"Maybe Cara didn't feel well and went home to rest," Mr. Bobbsey suggested.

"But she would have called," Mr. Farman insisted. "Besides, Laurel called her home a number of times. There was no answer. Then she went by and knocked for a long time. No one came to the door. She even looked in the windows."

Mr. Farman shook his head slowly. "It looks as if Cara Lassiter has really disappeared!"

4

Creepier and Creepier

The next morning after breakfast, the twins went to Creepy Castle with Mr. Farman. Laurel James was waiting for them on the drawbridge.

"Has Cara shown up?" Mr. Farman asked as the group walked toward the castle.

"No," the special-effects expert replied. "I called her house this morning. There was no answer. I went ahead and opened up as usual. I hope that was all right."

"Of course. You're in charge for now," Mr. Farman said.

"What about the police?" Freddie asked as they entered the castle. "Has anybody told them Cara is gone?"

"Not yet," Laurel said. "Mr. Farman and I thought it was too soon to file a missing persons report. But where could she be?"

"Maybe she never left the castle at all," Freddie said.

"Yeah," Flossie added. "Maybe she's locked up in a secret dungeon."

"Now, now," Mr. Farman said. "Let's not let our imaginations run away with us."

"I saw Cara leave yesterday afternoon," said Laurel.

"Did she say where she was going?" asked Nan.

Laurel shook her head. "I didn't speak to her. She was walking down the road toward the parking lot. I wish I had called to her."

By now they had reached the office. Laurel unlocked the door and pushed it open.

Mr. Farman turned to the twins. "Laurel and I have some business to discuss. Why don't you kids do some exploring?" he said.

"But we—" Freddie began. Then he felt Nan's elbow in his ribs and shut up.

"Sure," Nan said quickly. "Come on, you guys."

"What's the matter?" Freddie asked after they'd left the office. "I wanted to ask some more questions about Cara."

"Mr. Farman didn't want us hanging around," Nan replied. She led the others down the hallway. "Besides, remember what was happening yesterday morning when we came up here?"

"Cara and Laurel were having an argument," Flossie said. "Laurel said she was quitting."

"Right," said Bert. "And now she doesn't have to. Cara's gone and Laurel's in charge."

The twins came to a twisting stone stairway.

"Let's find out where these stairs go," said Freddie. He raced up the steps with the other twins following.

At the top, they found themselves in a narrow corridor. Wall lamps gave off a dim light.

Suddenly the twins heard faint noises behind them. They turned and froze.

Two huge figures were floating down the hall in their direction. One looked like a clown, and the other was a sea serpent.

The twins started to back away, but the figures kept floating toward them. Insane laughter filled the hallway. Then the figures faded into the stone walls.

The twins stood still for a moment.

"What was *that?*" Nan said finally.

"I think they were holograms," Freddie said with a gulp.

"What kind of grams?" asked Flossie.

"Holograms," Freddie repeated. "They're special effects, like three-dimensional pictures."

"They were pretty amazing," Bert said.

All of a sudden Flossie grabbed his arm. Farther down the hall a section of the stone wall was slowly swinging inward. Smoky reddish light streamed through the opening.

After a moment of silence, Bert said, "I think we're supposed to look inside."

"Just don't ask me to go in there," Flossie said. "What if the wall shuts again? We'll be trapped forever!"

Nan cleared her throat. "This is a fun house, remember?"

She started down the corridor. Freddie was right behind her. Flossie held on to Bert's arm.

The twins peered into a small room. It was filled with drifting red smoke. In the center of the room, two people sat at a chess table. One was dressed in a long black robe with a hood. The other looked like a skeleton.

"They're actors," Nan said.

At the sound of her voice, the figure in the robe turned toward them. Freddie gasped and edged closer to Nan. Was it just a trick of the light, or was the hood of the robe really empty?

The skeleton looked in their direction, too.

His eyes glared at them. Then he raised a bony hand. With a low groan, the section of wall swung closed.

"Wow!" said Bert. "That was pretty creepy."

"I'm scared," Flossie said.

"You know what?" said Freddie. "That skeleton reminded me of someone."

"I know!" Flossie cried. "The tall guy at the lake yesterday—Rick! He was glaring at us just like that."

"You mean the guy you said yelled at you for splashing?" Nan asked.

"Right," said Freddie.

"I'm tired of being scared," Flossie said. "When do we start having fun?"

Laughing, Bert reached over and rumpled her hair. "Just stick with me, kid," he said. Then he led the twins to the end of the corridor.

Around the corner was another flight of stone steps. The stairs went up and up in a spiral. Once again Freddie ran ahead.

"This must be the top floor of the castle," he called back to the others. "There's a window— Aieee!"

The floor was starting to tilt under his feet. An instant later Freddie was sliding faster and faster down a dark, winding tunnel.

A large bright circle appeared in front of

him. Freddie shot through it and landed in a room filled with foam balls. He tried to stand up, but he couldn't. It was a little like wearing roller skates on an icy sidewalk.

"Eeeee!" Suddenly Flossie came flying down and landed near him. Freddie laughed and threw an armful of foam balls at her.

"Look out below!" Bert called. Soon he, too, was scrambling around in the sea of foam.

Nan was close behind him. "This is great!" she exclaimed. She staggered to her feet, then stumbled and fell on top of Flossie.

"Hey, watch it," Flossie said.

"I wonder where we are?" Nan said. She half crawled, half swam across the little room toward the single window and looked out.

The drawbridge was right below her. People were waiting in line to enter Creepy Castle. A few people were leaving, too. One of them was a bald man wearing a bright blue-and-gray checked suit. He looked familiar. Wasn't that Mr. Phillips, the druggist?

Halfway across the drawbridge, the man stopped to check his wristwatch. Then he hurried down the road toward the parking lot.

Nan turned away from the window. Bert, Flossie, and Freddie were still falling around in the foam balls. She let out a yell and joined them.

After playing in the foam-ball room awhile, the twins decided it was time to go find Mr. Farman. At one end of the room they found a door leading to a hallway. By following the signs with arrows, they made their way to the office. Mr. Farman was still there, talking to Laurel James.

He looked up. "Having a good time?" he asked.

"We sure are," Freddie replied. "We went down a slide and ended up in a room full of balls."

Mr. Farman laughed. "That's a favorite of mine," he said.

The telephone rang. Laurel picked it up. As she listened, her face turned pale. She said a few words in a low voice and hung up.

"That was Edna Phillips, the druggist's wife," she said. "Mr. Phillips closed the drugstore early last night and never came home. His car is still parked behind the drugstore. She's been calling everyone she knows, but no one's seen him."

"Has she checked the hospitals?" Mr. Farman asked.

Laurel nodded. "There's no trace of him."

She took a deep breath and added, "Mrs. Phillips is afraid that her husband has been kidnapped!"

5

Missing Persons

"First Cara, and now Doug Phillips." Mr. Farman shook his head. "Two people disappearing in one day! I think it's time to call the police."

"Excuse me," Nan said. "But—"

"It's a little soon, isn't it?" Laurel interrupted. "I mean, there might be some simple explanation."

Mr. Farman frowned. "Maybe so. But if we wait to notify the police, the trail may get cold."

He reached for the telephone and dialed Sergeant Blandsford. Mr. Farman and the sergeant talked for a few minutes. Then Mr. Farman hung up. "He'll be here soon," he told the others.

When Sergeant Blandsford arrived, he took notes as Mr. Farman and Laurel told him what they knew about the two disappearances.

"I see," Sergeant Blandsford said when they had finished. "Do you mind if I use the phone? I want to call Edna Phillips and ask her a few more questions."

"Please help yourself," Mr. Farman replied.

While the policeman was on the phone, Nan started to tell Mr. Farman and Laurel about seeing Mr. Phillips that morning. But before she could get the words out, Sergeant Blandsford hung up. "That's funny," he said. "According to Mrs. Phillips, one of her husband's friends saw him late yesterday. He was on his way up here, to Creepy Castle. That's the last anyone saw of him."

Nan said quickly, "I think I saw him this morning."

Laurel glared at her. "Why didn't you say so earlier?"

"Never mind that," Mr. Farman said. "Go ahead, Nan. What happened?"

Nan told them about looking out the window and seeing the druggist leave the castle. "There were people in line waiting to get in," she finished. "Maybe some of them saw him, too."

"Could be," Sergeant Blandsford said. "But a lot of them were probably tourists. They might not have recognized Mr. Phillips even if they noticed him."

"You're sure he was walking away from the castle?" Laurel asked. When Nan nodded, Laurel sighed with relief. "Then wherever he vanished from, it wasn't here."

"But somebody saw him coming here yesterday afternoon," Freddie pointed out. "Does that mean he spent the night here?"

Laurel frowned. "I guess it's possible," she said slowly.

"I bet he hid in a secret dungeon," Freddie said.

Bert rolled his eyes. "You and your secret dungeons," he said.

Freddie looked hurt. "Well, why not? Don't creepy castles always have secret dungeons?"

Sergeant Blandsford put his hand on Freddie's arm to silence him. "Tell me, Nan," he said. "Did you get a good look at Mr. Phillips when he was leaving the castle?"

"Not really," Nan admitted. "I didn't see his face at all. But I recognized his checked jacket and his bald head."

Mr. Farman laughed. "That suit of his! I'd recognize it from half a mile away!"

The policeman closed his notebook. "Well, I'll ask around and see if anybody else saw him—and Ms. Lassiter, too, of course."

After Sergeant Blandsford left, Mr. Farman turned to the Bobbseys. "If you kids can help us solve these mysteries, we'd really appreciate it," he said. "It would be terrible if everyone started thinking of Creepy Castle as a place where people disappear."

"That wouldn't be fair," Laurel said. "Cara didn't vanish while she was in the castle. Neither did Mr. Phillips."

Mr. Farman shook his head. "It doesn't matter. Cara is the castle's general manager. Doug Phillips was last seen near here."

"We'll do our best, Mr. Farman," Bert said.

Mr. Farman smiled. "Thanks. I thought you'd say that. Oh, I almost forgot—we're supposed to have a cookout in the yard this afternoon. I'd better get home and start that charcoal. Laurel," he said, "call me if anything comes up. And if you hear from Cara, tell her to get in touch with me at once. I'm going to want an explanation."

The twins and Mr. Farman left the castle. Flossie was ahead of the others as they walked over the drawbridge. She glanced back over her shoulder for another look at the castle—and

bumped right into a stocky man with a cane. He had thick black hair and bushy eyebrows.

The man stepped back: "Hey, watch where you're going," he said.

"Oh, hello, Jeremy," Mr. Farman called. He came up with the others. "Have you seen Doug anywhere today?"

The stocky man scowled. "No," he said. "And I don't care if I never see that crook again."

Then he walked away, leaning on his cane.

"What a grouch!" Flossie exclaimed. "Who was that guy?"

"His name is Jeremy Hacker," Mr. Farman replied. "He's Mr. Phillips's partner at the drugstore."

"It sounds as if they don't get along very well," said Nan.

Mr. Farman nodded. "They can't agree on how to run the business, I suppose. I know Doug wants to buy Jeremy's share of the place, but Jeremy wants a lot of money for it." He thought for a moment. "You know, maybe Doug is off somewhere trying to raise some money. He might not want people to know what he's doing."

"Would he go off at night?" Flossie asked.

"Without telling his wife?" asked Nan.

"And without his car?" Freddie asked.

"Okay, okay," Mr. Farman said with a laugh. "I can see why you kids are the detectives instead of me. Come on, let's go back to the house and see about that cookout!"

Melissa and her parents had been invited to lunch, too. Later, Melissa and the Bobbseys played a round-robin series of badminton games. Melissa and Freddie came out on top. Then Melissa's parents invited the Bobbsey family to join them at a band concert on the common that evening.

"Why, thank you. That sounds delightful," Mrs. Bobbsey said.

Nan turned to Bert. "When are we supposed to start our investigation?" she said in a low voice.

He shrugged. "The whole town will probably be at the concert," he said. "Maybe we can question people between numbers."

When they got to the common that night, it looked as if everyone in Merlin *was* there. Melissa's parents found a large spot on the grass and spread out blankets for everyone to sit on. Mr. Farman produced a big bag of fresh popcorn from his knapsack. Flossie quickly sat next to him.

The musicians were already on the bandstand, tuning up. A few moments later the conductor came out. He bowed to the audience and raised his baton. The band started to play a rousing march.

By intermission the popcorn bag was empty.

"I'm thirsty," Flossie said.

"Me too," said Freddie.

Mr. Bobbsey handed Bert some money. "Why don't you and Nan buy sodas for everyone?"

"Thanks, Dad," Bert said. He and Nan headed toward the soft-drink stand.

After buying the sodas, Nan and Bert began walking back to the blanket. Nan lost sight of Bert in the crowd. Then she heard someone say "Doug Phillips" in a nasty voice. She looked around.

Jeremy Hacker, the man whom Flossie had bumped into that morning, was standing a few feet away. He was talking to a small group of men. Nan stopped to listen.

"He couldn't take the pressure," Mr. Hacker said. "So he ran away. Now I've got to step in and keep the store going."

"Doug won't like that one bit," someone remarked.

"He doesn't have to like it. He isn't around,"

Mr. Hacker said. "And for all I know he's gone for good. Now I can—"

Just then Jeremy Hacker looked up and saw Nan watching him. He stopped talking, and his eyes blazed with fury.

"You little snoop," he said, coming over. He shook his cane in Nan's face. "What do you mean by spying on me? Listen, and listen good. If I catch you snooping again, you'll regret it for a long, long time!"

6

Spying on Suspects

Nan backed away from the angry man.

Then she heard the audience start to clap. She glanced over at the bandstand. In another moment, the next part of the program would begin.

Nan wanted to leave, but Mr. Hacker was blocking her way.

"Uh, excuse me," Nan muttered. Still glaring, Mr. Hacker stepped aside. Nan hurried over to the blanket. She sat down just as the band started to play.

"Where have you been?" Bert whispered. "I thought you'd gotten lost."

"Not exactly," she whispered back. "I—"

Someone on a nearby blanket said, "Shhh!"

When the piece was over, Nan quickly told Bert, Flossie, and Freddie what had happened.

"Mr. Hacker's trying to hide something," Nan said. "But what? Did he have something to do with Mr. Phillips's disappearance?"

"We saw him at Creepy Castle this morning," Bert said. "And you saw Mr. Phillips there, too. Maybe they were having a meeting at the castle."

"Why meet at a fun house?" Flossie asked.

Bert shrugged. "Maybe they didn't want anybody to know they were getting together."

"Quiet," Freddie warned. "The music's starting again. We'll talk later."

After they'd returned to Mr. Farman's, the twins got together in Nan and Flossie's room to discuss the case.

"Cara Lassiter and Mr. Phillips are both missing," Nan said. "But how do we know there's a connection?"

Freddie rolled his eyes. "Two people vanish around Creepy Castle on practically the same day? Of course there's a connection!"

"Okay, but what is it?" asked Bert.

Flossie's eyes grew wide. "The vampire!" she said. "The one who lives at Creepy Castle. *He* grabbed Cara and Mr. Phillips."

"Ooo-o-o," Freddie moaned. He raised his

hands like claws on either side of his head and made a scary face. "And now . . . he's waiting for *us!*"

Flossie let out a little squeak.

"Come on, guys," Bert said. "Get serious."

"I *am* serious," Flossie insisted. "And I saw a mysterious vampire, didn't I?"

"You *say* you did," Freddie muttered.

Flossie ignored her twin. "So the vampire must have kidnapped Cara and Mr. Phillips and taken them to his secret lair."

"But both Cara and Mr. Phillips were seen leaving the castle," Nan pointed out.

"I have a funny feeling about Laurel James," said Bert. "She had a big argument with Cara Lassiter the same day Cara vanished. And we have only her word that Cara left the castle."

"But what about Mr. Phillips?" Nan asked.

Bert hesitated. "Maybe he saw something," he said finally. "So Laurel had to kidnap him, too."

Nan thought it over. "I don't know. Maybe that mean Mr. Hacker kidnapped Mr. Phillips so he could take over the drugstore."

"But why would Mr. Hacker kidnap Cara?" Flossie asked.

Nan frowned and shook her head. "Maybe

he didn't. Maybe Cara really *did* go away on her own."

"That's pretty hard to believe," Freddie said.

Bert raised one hand. "Okay, okay! Look, tomorrow morning we'll split into teams. Nan, you and Freddie can check out Laurel. Flossie and I will take a closer look at Mr. Hacker."

"Not too close," Nan warned. "That guy has a really bad temper."

After breakfast the next morning, Nan and Freddie rode their rented bicycles up to the castle.

Bert and Flossie headed into town. They parked their bikes in front of Phillips's Drugstore and went in. The store looked empty, but they heard voices from the back room. One of them sounded like Jeremy Hacker.

"You get the point?" he was saying. "I'm in charge now. And if you don't like it . . ."

"No, no, Mr. Hacker." The other man sounded a little frightened. "It's just—well, what do I tell Mr. Phillips when he comes back?"

Jeremy Hacker gave an ugly laugh. "*If* he comes back, you mean," he said. "Any more questions before I go?"

"No, sir."

A moment later Bert and Flossie heard a door slam.

"I bet Mr. Hacker left by the back," Bert said. "Come on, let's follow him!"

They hurried outside and looked for a way to get behind the drugstore. Finally Flossie spotted an alley on the side street. They were about to start down it when a car appeared, heading straight toward them.

"Out of the way," Bert said quickly. They ducked into a doorway. The driver turned left and sped out of sight.

"That was Mr. Hacker!" Flossie exclaimed. "I got a good look at his face."

"That's not all," Bert said grimly. "I saw something large in the backseat. It was covered with a blanket."

"I bet it was Mr. Phillips!" cried Flossie. "Mr. Hacker must be taking him someplace to hide him."

"But where?" said Bert. He thought for a minute. "Maybe Mr. Hacker's taking Mr. Phillips to his house." He looked across the street at the common. Melissa was on the swings in the playground. "Melissa might know where he lives," Bert told Flossie.

They hurried over to the common and told Melissa what they wanted and why.

"Sure, I can take you there," Melissa said. "But I'd better warn you—Mr. Hacker hates kids. If he catches us, we're in big trouble."

Meanwhile, Nan and Freddie were talking to Laurel James.

"The control room is off limits to the public," Laurel said. "Why do you kids want to see it?"

"Mr. Farman asked us to find out more about Cara's disappearance," Nan said. "We'd like to see the control room as part of our investigation."

Laurel sighed. "Okay. But not for long. Now that Cara's gone, I've got a million things to do."

She led them to a private part of the castle. Then they went through an unmarked door and down a flight of stairs. Freddie noticed a thumping noise. It got louder as they went down the stairs.

"What's that sound?" he asked nervously.

Laurel looked back at Freddie. "The noise? Oh, I don't know," she said. "It's probably the pump that keeps the cellar from getting flooded."

She pushed open a door. "Here we are."

"Wow!" Freddie stepped in and looked

around, wide-eyed. TV monitors covered one wall. Each one showed a different section of the castle. Freddie saw the front entrance, the Mirror Maze, the room full of foam balls, and many others.

Under the monitors was a control panel. Laurel sat on a chair in front of it.

"Most of our special effects are controlled by computer," she explained.

"Then what do all these knobs and switches do?" asked Nan.

"They let me control the effects without the computer," Laurel said. "I can also use the panel to develop new special effects. I could make Creepy Castle *really* scary. But Mr. Farman and Cara say it has to stay funny."

Nan glanced up at the monitors again. Someone was walking through the Mirror Maze—someone in a long black cape. "Freddie, look!" she said. "That must be Flossie's vampire!"

As if he had heard Nan's words, the figure turned. He stared in the direction of the hidden camera. The white face, dark eyes, and pointed teeth were unmistakable. Freddie noticed an ugly scar on the vampire's left cheek.

Suddenly, with a swirl of his cape, the vam-

pire walked right *into* a mirror. Then he vanished.

"That was really amazing!" Freddie said. "How did you do that?"

"I didn't," Laurel said. Her face was pale. Beads of sweat dotted her forehead. "That wasn't a special effect. That was real!"

7

Big Surprises

"I've never seen that vampire before," Laurel said. "I'm going to get to the bottom of this." She jumped up and started for the door.

Nan exchanged a look with Freddie. "Come on," she said, "let's go."

They followed Laurel up the stairs and along the hallway. Laurel entered the Mirror Maze. She turned one way and then another. Nan and Freddie stayed right behind her.

Laurel stopped suddenly. She pointed to the mirrored ceiling. "The TV camera is right up there. Whoever that was must have been right about here."

"But how did he disappear?" Nan asked. She looked around. Was this the same place where

Flossie had seen the vampire? All the mirrors made it hard to tell.

Nan bent down to look at the floor. It was marked with long scratches, as if something heavy had been dragged across it. But Nan could find no sign of any opening.

"Are you looking for a trapdoor?" asked Freddie.

Nan nodded. "Right."

"We do have some trapdoors at Creepy Castle," Laurel said. "But none of them are in this part of the castle."

Nan tapped the edges of the mirrors. She wanted to see if any of them opened like a door. None of them moved.

"I think I have the answer," Freddie said.

Laurel looked at him in surprise. "Oh?"

Freddie swallowed. "We just saw the ghost of Mr. Horvath. You know, the vampire actor who built this place."

Laurel laughed, but a shiver ran down Nan's spine. Was a ghost watching them from behind one of the mirrors?

Melissa stopped her bike at the top of a small hill. Flossie and Bert pulled up next to her.

"That's Jeremy Hacker's place," Melissa said. She pointed to an old house below.

Behind the house was a small shed. In the

driveway was the car Bert and Flossie had seen at the drugstore.

"This place looks kind of run-down," Flossie said. "Why doesn't Mr. Hacker fix it up?"

"Maybe he's too cheap to spend the money," Melissa replied.

Bert snorted. "He sounds like an all-around nice guy," he said. "Let's go down there."

"Okay, but we can't let him see us," Melissa said.

They hid their bikes in a ditch at the bottom of the hill. Bert led the way toward the back of the house. Then Flossie saw him suddenly crouch behind a bush. He motioned for her and Melissa to do the same.

Flossie and Melissa crept up to Bert. Flossie pulled back a branch so she could see. Jeremy Hacker was crossing the backyard to the shed. He was carrying a bunch of keys in one hand. In the other was a plate of food.

"Bert!" Flossie whispered.

"Sssh," Bert said. "He'll hear us!"

Mr. Hacker put down the plate and unlocked the shed door. Then he took the food inside. A minute later he came out without the plate. Finally he locked the door again.

The moment Mr. Hacker was back inside his house Flossie grabbed Bert's arm. "He was taking food to Mr. Phillips! Mr. Hacker kidnapped him and locked him up in that shed! We've got to get the police!"

"Not until we're sure," Bert replied.

Melissa frowned. "But how—"

"We've got to see inside that shed," Bert said.

"Look, there's a window that's partly open," Flossie said. "It's awfully high off the ground, though."

Bert looked up at the window. "What if I give you a boost? Could you look in?"

Flossie gulped. "Um—I guess so. . . . I don't have to go inside, do I?"

"No way," Bert said firmly. "Just take a look. Then we'll head back to town. Ready?"

Bert stood up and ran across the yard to the shed. Flossie followed right behind him. Melissa stayed on guard in the bushes.

When Bert and Flossie reached the shed, Bert wrapped his arms around Flossie's knees. With a grunt he lifted her up. Flossie grabbed the windowsill.

The inside of the shed was dark. Flossie leaned closer to the half-open window. She shaded her eyes with her hand. Was something moving in the corner?

"Mr. Phillips!" she called softly. "Mr. Phillips, is that you?"

No answer. Flossie squinted into the darkness. Something was moving. It came to-

ward her quickly but silently. Then it leapt up at the window.

Flossie pulled her head back but not in time. A long pink tongue licked her cheek.

"Yikes!" she cried, letting go of the windowsill. She felt herself start to tumble backward.

"Watch out," Bert said. He staggered back a few steps, then he dropped Flossie to the ground.

A loud bark came from the shed.

"That's sure not Mr. Phillips," Bert said.

"Nope." Flossie giggled. "It's a dog."

"Hey, you kids!" Jeremy Hacker shouted from the back door of the house. "What are you doing in my yard? Get out of here!"

"Good idea," Bert muttered. He grabbed Flossie's hand, and they ran toward the bushes. Melissa was still hiding there. A few moments later the three of them were pedaling their bikes away as fast as they could.

"Let's stay here in the Mirror Maze," Nan said to Freddie. Laurel had given up looking for the vampire. She'd gone back to the office.

Freddie hesitated. What if the vampire showed up again? "Why?" he asked.

"I want to take another look at those scratches I found," Nan said.

Freddie straightened his shoulders. He was a pretty tough detective! "Sure, Nan," he said.

Nan knelt down and felt the scratches on the floor.

"I'll be back in a minute," Freddie said. "I want to see what's over that way."

"Okay," Nan said without looking up. "Don't get lost."

Three or four turns later, Freddie realized he *was* lost. Well, it was a maze, wasn't it? He kept on going. Soon he was even more confused.

Suddenly Freddie walked right into someone in a dark suit. Freddie looked up and recognized the man from the lake. He was Rick, one of the actors.

"Sorry," Freddie said.

Rick scowled in reply.

Freddie saw that Rick's fingers were covered with dark green makeup. "Were you being a green monster?" he asked.

"What?" Rick looked down at his fingers. Quickly he whipped out a tissue and started cleaning them. The makeup didn't come off. "That's right, kid," he said in a gruff voice. "But don't tell anybody I told you. It's against the rules."

"Oh, I won't," Freddie said. Maybe Rick wasn't such a mean guy after all.

Rick walked away, and Freddie decided to

follow him. Freddie figured Rick would know the shortest path out of the maze.

A few turns later Freddie realized that something about Rick's face had been familiar. Suddenly he remembered. The scar! There had been a scar on the vampire's face, too. He'd seen it on the monitor. Freddie's eyes widened.

Of course! The vampire wasn't the ghost of Mr. Horvath at all. Rick was a real vampire!

Up ahead, Rick had reached the end of the maze. He opened an unmarked door and stepped through.

Freddie hesitated. Should he keep following Rick? Or should he turn back and try to find Nan? He really didn't feel like entering the maze again. Freddie took a deep breath and walked through the door.

He found himself in a long, empty hallway. After the glaring lights of the maze, it seemed very dim and gloomy. And where was Rick?

Freddie started down the hall. Then he heard a funny noise behind him—it was a high-pitched squeak. Freddie looked over his shoulder and froze.

A gigantic purple bat with glowing green eyes was flying down the hallway. It was heading straight at him!

8

Going Nowhere

Freddie turned and ran. The hallway seemed endless. Was the giant bat catching up to him? He was afraid to look. His legs ached, and he was getting a pain in his side.

"Oof!" Freddie tripped over his own feet and tumbled to the floor. He scrunched his eyes shut. What would it feel like to be attacked by a giant bat? He really didn't want to find out.

Freddie lay on the floor and waited. At any moment he expected to feel the bat's hot breath on his neck. Nothing happened. Finally Freddie opened his eyes and raised his head. The hallway was empty. No gigantic bat, no vampire, nothing.

He sat up and rubbed his knee where it had hit the floor. "I *did* see a bat," he said out loud.

Then Freddie remembered what Laurel had said in the control room. The special effects in the castle were set off by computers. He got to his feet and walked slowly back down the hall. As he went, he looked carefully at the walls. In the middle of the hall he stopped.

Sure enough, there were tiny holes in the wall on both sides of the hall. Freddie took a deep breath. He waved his hand in front of one of the holes. At first nothing happened. Then the high-pitched squeaks started again.

This time Freddie knew what to expect. But he couldn't help ducking when the gigantic bat appeared in midair. It swooped down the hall-way and vanished.

Freddie sighed in relief. The bat must be a hologram, he told himself. Just like those mon-sters.

He decided to keep going down the hallway. Then he heard Nan calling his name, so he turned back.

Nan had just come out of the door from the maze.

"Where have you been?" she demanded. "I thought I'd lost you."

"I was following that guy Rick," Freddie said. "Then I got attacked by a giant bat. It turned out to be a hologram, but it really scared me. You know what, though? Rick is a real vampire."

"What do you mean?" Nan asked.

Freddie told her about the scar on Rick's face. "So that proves it," he said.

"Oh, Freddie," Nan said, laughing. "A vampire who swims in a lake? In the *daytime?* Besides, Flossie didn't say that the vampire she saw had a scar."

Freddie ignored her. "There's something I can't figure out, though. Rick had dark green makeup on his fingers. But vampires aren't dark green. Have we seen any dark green monsters yet?"

"I don't think so," Nan said with a shrug. "But we probably haven't run into all the monsters in this place yet."

"Right." Freddie grinned. "Hey, you want to see something neat? Walk down this hallway."

A moment later Nan was ducking as the giant purple bat swooped down at her. "You creep, Freddie Bobbsey!" she shouted. "I'll get you for this!"

Bert and Melissa stopped at the edge of the common. Flossie pulled her bike up next to them.

"I have to go home now," Melissa was saying. "See you later, okay?" She waved as she rode off.

Flossie watched Melissa go. Suddenly she saw a red-haired woman in a red T-shirt and jeans come out of a store across the street. The woman was wearing big sunglasses with yellow frames.

"Bert, look!" Flossie said. "Isn't that Cara Lassiter?"

As Flossie spoke, the woman turned into the drugstore.

"I couldn't really see her," Bert said. "But she *did* look like Cara."

"Maybe she just went off somewhere, and now she's back," Flossie said. "I guess there isn't any mystery after all."

Bert frowned. "Wait, there she is again. She's going into the grocery store on the corner right now."

"She must have errands to do," Flossie said.

"It looks that way," Bert agreed. "Listen, Floss. I'm pretty thirsty. Why don't you go into the grocery store and buy us a couple of sodas?"

"Why don't *you*—" Flossie began. Then she stopped herself. "Oh, you mean go over there and check Cara out? Sure!"

She quickly crossed the street and entered the grocery store. The red-haired woman was at the back, near the soft-drink cooler. Flossie walked past her.

The woman's face looked a little familiar. But the big dark glasses made it hard to tell if she was really Cara Lassiter.

"Excuse me," Flossie said. She walked over and slid open the cooler door.

The woman turned away, heading toward the check-out counter. Flossie grabbed three cans of soda and hurried after her.

"Will that be all?" the clerk was asking.

"That's right," the woman said. She unsnapped her purse and pulled out a new twenty-dollar bill. Another one was stuck to it.

Flossie's eyes widened. In the woman's purse was a whole stack of crisp twenty-dollar bills. She was carrying a fortune!

The woman glanced down and saw Flossie. She quickly snapped her purse shut.

Flossie gave her a big smile. "You work at Creepy Castle, don't you?" she asked.

"No," the woman said. She picked up her bag of groceries and hurried toward the side door.

Flossie started after her.

"Hey, what about those sodas?" the clerk called.

"Sorry," Flossie said. She pulled some money

from her pocket and paid. By the time she got to the side door, the red-haired woman was nowhere in sight.

Flossie hurried around the corner and across the street to Bert. "Did you see her?" she demanded. "She went out the side door."

Bert clapped a hand to his head. "Oh, no!" he said. "I forgot about the side door! I can't see it from here. She must have gone the other way."

Suddenly he frowned. "Hey, look—there's Lily, the woman we saw at the lake the other day. Isn't she an actress at the castle?"

Flossie looked back across the street. The woman had short dark hair. She, too, was wearing jeans and a red T-shirt. "That's Lily all right," Flossie said.

"She's probably on her way to work," Bert said. Lily stepped into her green station wagon and sped away.

Bert thought for a minute. Then he climbed onto his bike. "Let's go up to Creepy Castle, Floss. I want to find out more about Lily. She and the woman who looked like Cara Lassiter were wearing the same clothes!"

Flossie hopped on her bike and pedaled after Bert to the castle. They showed their passes and went inside. Laurel James was coming out of the office. She looked very upset.

"Is anything wrong?" Bert asked.

Laurel shrugged. "Nothing much," she replied. "But a few of our actors seem to be taking the day off. And somebody else saw that vampire thing near the Mirror Maze."

"*My* vampire?" Flossie asked eagerly.

"Well, if he's yours, take him home with you," Laurel said crossly. "He's just another problem for me to deal with. I never knew that managing this place was so much work. I wish Cara would come back."

"Have you seen Nan and Freddie?" Bert asked.

"They're in the north wing," Laurel said. "They wanted to see some parts of the castle that aren't open to the public yet. Come on, I'll show you where to go."

At the end of a short hallway, Laurel opened a door marked No Entry.

"Down to the end and turn right," she said. "You should find them without any trouble."

"Thanks," Bert said. He started down the corridor with Flossie close behind him.

Flossie wrinkled her nose. "It smells terrible here. Like wet old washcloths."

"This part of the castle has probably been shut up for years," said Bert.

They turned right, into another dimly lit hallway.

"I don't like this part," Flossie said. "The walls are all crumbly."

"Come on, Floss," Bert replied. "We need to find Freddie and Nan."

"There they are," Flossie said. "Hey, you guys!" she called loudly.

Nan and Freddie waved from the end of the long hall. Bert walked faster. He couldn't wait to tell them about seeing Lily and Cara. Maybe Nan and Freddie had found some clues, too.

"Hey, what—" The stone floor suddenly tilted under Bert's feet. He was dumped onto a curved wooden slide. Then he went flying down through darkness.

9

Splashdown!

"Come on!" Nan cried, breaking into a run. "Bert's in trouble!"

Flossie was kneeling on the edge of the opening in the floor. She stared down into the blackness. When she looked up at Nan, her lower lip was trembling. "I heard a splash," she said.

"Bert!" Nan yelled down. "Are you okay?"

A moment later Bert's voice called faintly, "Yes! I'm in some sort of pool!"

"We have to save him!" wailed Flossie.

Nan turned to the younger twins. "Now, listen, you two," she said. "Go to the office, find Laurel, and tell her what happened. We need her help."

"What about you?" Freddie asked.

"I'm going down there," Nan said. "Now, move it!"

Freddie and Flossie ran back down the hall.

Nan lowered herself through the trapdoor. There was some kind of slide underneath her. She held on to the sides, to slow herself.

"I'm coming down!" Nan called to Bert.

"Watch out," he called back. "It's deep."

Suddenly the slide got steeper. Nan sailed through the air. She had just enough time to take a deep breath. Then she hit the dark, cold water.

Nan sank down deeper and deeper. Then she felt her feet touch the bottom. She tried to swim to the surface, but her sneakers and jeans were dragging her down. For a moment Nan thought she couldn't do it. Then her head broke through the water. She gulped for air.

"Nan! Over here," Bert called.

Nan pushed the wet hair away from her eyes. She couldn't see anything at all. Nan swam quickly toward Bert's voice. Finally her hand touched his shoulder. Bert was holding on to the tiled edge of the pool.

"Next time I'll wear my bathing suit," Nan joked.

Suddenly a door crashed open and the lights went on. Nan and Bert could see that they were in a large tiled room. Laurel came running toward the pool, followed by Freddie and Flossie. "Thank goodness you're safe!" Laurel cried.

Nan climbed out of the pool. Her shorts and shirt were stuck to her skin.

"Could you give me a hand?" Bert asked Laurel. "I think I twisted my wrist."

Laurel knelt down and helped Bert out of the pool. He sat on the edge and gingerly felt his wrist. "It just aches a little," he said.

"That trapdoor is really dangerous," said Nan. "What if we couldn't swim?"

Laurel shook her head. "I'm so sorry. I completely forgot about the trapdoor," she said. "We keep the pool clean, but Mr. Farman hasn't decided what to do with it yet. Mr. Horvath liked to invite his guests for a swim. Then he'd surprise them with that trapdoor."

"Some joke," Bert said. He emptied the water from his sneakers and put them back on.

"I think we'd better get back to Mr. Farman's," Nan said to the other twins. "Bert and I need dry clothes."

"And we haven't had lunch yet," Flossie added. "I'm starved."

The twins said goodbye to Laurel and left the castle. As soon as they reached Mr. Farman's house, Nan and Bert went upstairs to change.

Flossie and Freddie quickly made some sandwiches. Then all the twins took their lunches out to the porch.

"We'd better talk about this mystery," Bert said.

Nan sat down on the swing. "I don't think the kidnapper is Laurel," she said. "She doesn't sound as if she wants to be in charge anymore."

"She was very worried about you and Bert when you fell into the pool," Flossie said.

"I still think the vampire kidnapped Cara and Mr. Phillips," Freddie said. "And I know who the vampire is, too." He told the others about seeing Rick in the maze. Then he turned to Flossie. "When you saw the vampire in the Mirror Maze, did he have a scar on his face?"

Flossie frowned. "I didn't notice," she said. "I guess I was too scared."

"I don't believe in vampires," Bert said. "But what about Mr. Hacker? Maybe he did kidnap Mr. Phillips, but he's not hiding him in that shed. I still don't know why Mr. Hacker would kidnap Cara, though."

"We're not even sure she was kidnapped," Flossie said. She told Nan and Freddie about the woman in the grocery store. Then Bert told them about seeing Lily.

"Was it really Cara?" Nan asked, frowning.

"Or maybe Lily was dressed up like Cara and wearing a wig. But why would Lily do that?"

Bert shrugged. "It *could* have been a coincidence that they were wearing the same clothes."

"Anyway," Nan said, "Creepy Castle is the key to this case. The last time Cara and Mr. Phillips were seen, they were in the castle."

"*Leaving* the castle," Bert pointed out. "You saw Mr. Phillips yourself."

"That's true," Nan agreed. "But what if they came back? What if they're somewhere inside?"

"In the vampire's lair," Freddie said in a spooky voice.

Nan ignored him. "I vote we go back to the castle now," she said. "How much time do we have before it closes? Half an hour?"

She glanced at her watch. Then she gasped. "Wait a minute," she said. "When I saw Mr. Phillips leaving the castle, he stopped and looked at his wristwatch. But Mr. Phillips has a pocket watch, remember? So that man wasn't Mr. Phillips!"

Bert frowned. "Then it was someone pretending to be him—to make people think that Mr. Phillips left the castle. But he didn't! He's still there!"

"That mirror in the maze," Freddie said. "I bet it leads to a secret room."

Bert sprang up. "What are we waiting for?" he said. "Let's get up there!"

All of the Bobbseys raced down the porch steps and jumped on their bikes. When they arrived at Creepy Castle, the front door was still open. The twins slipped inside.

The hallways were deserted. Nan led them through the Mirror Maze. They went straight to the spot with the marks on the floor.

"One of these mirrors must be a secret door," Bert said.

"That's what I thought," Nan said. "But how does it open?"

"Listen, what's that?" Flossie whispered.

Footsteps echoed in the distance. Then a door slammed. A *big* door. A moment later, all the lights went out.

"Oh, no!" Nan exclaimed in the sudden darkness. "We're locked in Creepy Castle for the night!"

10

Special Effects

Freddie tried to see something, anything, in the blackness. It was no use. "What'll we do?" he asked.

"No problem," Bert's voice said from somewhere to his left. "I have a pocket flashlight."

A narrow beam of light appeared, multiplied by the mirrors all around them.

"I don't want to spend the night in this scary old castle," Flossie wailed. "Can't we find a telephone somewhere? Mr. Farman can get us out."

"Good idea," Nan said. "Maybe the office—"

"Look!" Flossie gasped. "There's a person in the mirror!"

"I saw him, too," Freddie said. "But who is it?"

"Quiet, everybody," Bert whispered. "I'm turning off the flashlight. Maybe he didn't see us."

A faint light seemed to move toward them from behind the mirror. Then the mirror began to move. Flossie grabbed Bert's arm.

The mirror swung open, scraping on the floor. Rick appeared in the opening. He had a powerful flashlight in one hand and a suitcase in the other.

Freddie backed away, bumping into Bert. Bert's flashlight banged against one of the mirrors.

At the sound Rick whirled around and dashed back behind the mirror. Then the mirror began to close. Bert rushed over and jammed his flashlight in the crack.

"Come on!" he said. "If we all pull, I think we can open it."

The twins made their way over to Bert's side.

"One, two, *three*," Bert said.

At first nothing happened. Then the mirror swung open again. Bert's flashlight clattered to the floor.

He bent down and felt around for it. "I hope it's still working," he said.

A moment later Bert found the flashlight and flipped the switch. The beam cut through the darkness. Bert saw a flight of stone steps leading downward. "Rick must have gone that way," he said. "Let's go!"

At the bottom of the stairs was a closed door. The Bobbseys burst through. Bert swung his flashlight around the room. It had no windows. The only furniture was a couple of chairs and a sagging bed.

Flossie pointed to a corner. "What's that big thing over there?" she asked.

"Well, what do you know?" Bert said, moving closer. "It's a printing press. And it looks new!"

Nan clapped a hand to her head. "Freddie, remember that green makeup you saw on Rick's hand? That wasn't makeup. It was printer's ink."

Freddie picked up a crisp ten-dollar bill from the floor. "You mean he was—"

"Printing fake money," Nan finished.

Suddenly the twins heard a choking noise. It was coming from near the printing press.

Bert shone the flashlight in the direction of the noise. Two pairs of frightened eyes looked back at him.

Nan felt along the wall for a light switch. She

found one and flicked it. The room flooded with light. "It's Cara Lassiter and Mr. Phillips!" Bert said. "Quick, let's untie them!"

"Which way did Rick go?" Nan demanded as soon as the two prisoners were loose.

Cara cleared her throat and said, "He came running back and told that girl, Lily, that the cops were upstairs. They went out through the sliding panel over there." She pointed to the opposite side of the room.

"We've got to stop them," Bert said. "But how?"

"I know!" Freddie shouted. "The special effects! Cara, do you know how to run them?"

The castle manager nodded. "A few, anyway."

"How do we get to the control room from here?" Freddie asked excitedly.

"Through the panel," Cara replied. Quickly she crossed the room and pressed a switch in the corner. A section of the wall slid aside. Then she led the group down the hall, to the control room.

While Cara turned on the control board, Nan found a telephone. She called Sergeant Blandsford and told him what had happened.

"We'll be at the castle right away," the policeman said. "Be careful."

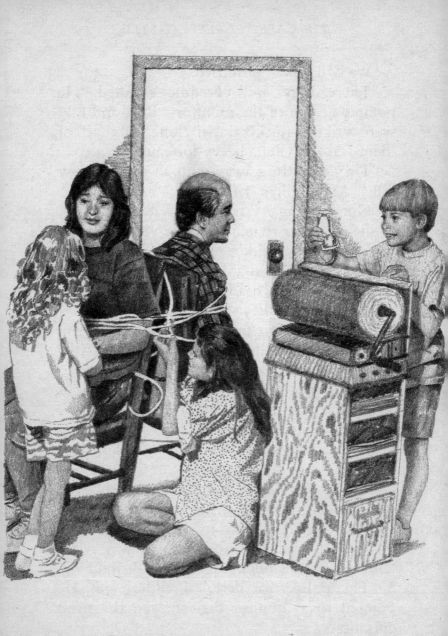

"We will," Nan promised.

"There they are!" Freddie shouted. He pointed at one of the monitors. Rick and Lily were walking quickly down a long hall. Each of them was carrying a heavy-looking suitcase.

"They're getting away with all those phony bills!" Mr. Phillips cried.

"Not for long," Cara said. "Watch this!"

She flipped a switch. A stone wall suddenly slid across the corridor, blocking it. She flipped another switch, and a door creaked open. But as Rick and Lily headed toward it, the floor tilted sideways. They tumbled to the ground.

As they rose to their feet, a green dragon breathing orange flames came flying up the hall. The crooks backed away. Rick managed to open a door behind him.

"Freddie, push button eight," Cara said.

Monitor eight showed Rick and Lily running up a long stairway. They were moving more slowly now.

Cara pressed another button. Suddenly the stairs folded down to make a long slide. Rick and Lily fell helplessly to the bottom. Then they got up and ran through a doorway. They left the suitcases full of fake money behind.

"The police are here," Freddie said. He pointed to a monitor that showed the front entrance.

"I'll let them in," Cara replied. She pressed another button. The big double doors swung open just as the two crooks reached the entrance. They ran right into the police officers. Moments later they were in handcuffs.

The Bobbseys, Cara, and Mr. Phillips cheered and hugged one another.

"We got 'em!" Flossie cried.

Bert grinned. "It was really the castle that got them!"

"Welcome to Creepy Castle," a hollow voice said. "We have been expecting you." Ghostly laughter filled the air.

The twins were at the castle the next evening for a special party in their honor.

The far end of the room began to fill with green smoke that took the shape of a giant head. Lightning flashed, and thunder echoed off the stone walls. Then the head spoke in a booming voice.

"Let the guests of honor come to the ballroom," it commanded.

The twins grinned at one another.

A door opened on the other side of the room. "I'll go first," Nan said. She stepped through and found herself sliding downward. "Whee!" she cried out. Her brothers and sister were right behind her.

Melissa, Cara, Laurel, and Mr. Phillips were already in the ballroom. So were the twins' parents and Mr. Farman. Tables with food had been set up, and Mr. Phillips was scooping ice cream out of a huge drum. The twins each took a large bowl.

"There's something I don't understand," Flossie said as they sat down. "If Mr. Hacker wasn't the kidnapper, why did he come to the castle that day?" She popped a big spoonful of ice cream into her mouth.

"I can answer that," said Laurel. "He had just bought a new computer. He wanted to talk to me about it."

"Maybe that's what we saw in his car," Bert told Flossie.

"But I still don't understand why Rick and Lily kidnapped *you*," Nan said to Cara.

"They knew I was getting suspicious of them," Cara replied. "So they grabbed me and locked me up. Then Lily walked out wearing a red wig. I guess she wanted to make people think I'd left the castle."

"Then she came to the drugstore," Mr. Phillips added. "She paid me with a phony bill. I didn't spot it at first. When I did, I followed her back here. I saw her take off the wig. They couldn't risk my spoiling their plans, so they grabbed me, too."

Nan nodded. "Then Rick put on your jacket and left the castle," she said. "His big mistake was using his wristwatch instead of your pocket watch."

"Oh, no, it wasn't," Cara said.

She raised her voice so that everyone in the room could hear. "His biggest mistake was tangling with the Bobbsey twins!"

NANCY DREW® MYSTERY STORIES By Carolyn Keene

THE TRIPLE HOAX—#57	69153	$3.50	_____
THE FLYING SAUCER MYSTERY—#58	65796	$3.50	_____
THE SECRET IN THE OLD LACE—#59	69067	$3.50	_____
THE GREEK SYMBOL MYSTERY—#60	67457	$3.50	_____
THE SWAMI'S RING—#61	62467	$3.50	_____
THE KACHINA DOLL MYSTERY—#62	67220	$3.50	_____
THE TWIN DILEMMA—#63	67301	$3.50	_____
CAPTIVE WITNESS—#64	62469	$3.50	_____
MYSTERY OF THE WINGED LION—#65	62681	$3.50	_____
RACE AGAINST TIME—#66	69485	$3.50	_____
THE SINISTER OMEN—#67	62471	$3.50	_____
THE ELUSIVE HEIRESS—#68	62478	$3.50	_____
CLUE IN THE ANCIENT DISGUISE—#69	64279	$3.50	_____
THE BROKEN ANCHOR—#70	62481	$3.50	_____
THE SILVER COBWEB—#71	62470	$3.50	_____
THE HAUNTED CAROUSEL—#72	66227	$3.50	_____
ENEMY MATCH—#73	64283	$3.50	_____
MYSTERIOUS IMAGE—#74	69401	$3.50	_____
THE EMERALD-EYED CAT MYSTERY—#75	64282	$3.50	_____
THE ESKIMO'S SECRET—#76	62468	$3.50	_____
THE BLUEBEARD ROOM—#77	66857	$3.50	_____
THE PHANTOM OF VENICE—#78	66230	$3.50	_____
THE DOUBLE HORROR OF FENLEY PLACE—#79	64387	$3.50	_____
THE CASE OF THE DISAPPEARING DIAMONDS—#80	64896	$3.50	_____
MARDI GRAS MYSTERY—#81	64961	$3.50	_____
THE CLUE IN THE CAMERA—#82	64962	$3.50	_____
THE CASE OF THE VANISHING VEIL—#83	63413	$3.50	_____
THE JOKER'S REVENGE—#84	63426	$3.50	_____
THE SECRET OF SHADY GLEN—#85	63416	$3.50	_____
THE MYSTERY OF MISTY CANYON—#86	63417	$3.50	_____
THE CASE OF THE RISING STARS—#87	66312	$3.50	_____
THE SEARCH FOR CINDY AUSTIN—#88	66313	$3.50	_____
THE CASE OF THE DISAPPEARING DEEJAY—#89	66314	$3.50	_____
THE PUZZLE AT PINEVIEW SCHOOL—#90	66315	$3.95	_____
THE GIRL WHO COULDN'T REMEMBER—#91	66316	$3.50	_____
THE GHOST OF CRAVEN COVE—#92	66317	$3.50	_____
THE SAFECRACKER'S SECRET—#93	66318	$3.50	_____
THE PICTURE PERFECT MYSTERY—#94	66311	$3.50	_____
NANCY DREW® GHOST STORIES—#1	46468	$3.50	_____

and don't forget...THE HARDY BOYS® Now available in paperback

MEET THE *NEW* BOBBSEY TWINS™
THE BOBBSEY TWINS ARE BACK
AND BETTER THAN EVER!

When older twins Nan and Bert and younger twins Freddie and Flossie get into mischief, there's no end to the mystery and adventure.

Join the Bobbsey twins as they track down clues, escape danger, and unravel mysteries in these brand-new, fun-filled stories.

The *New* Bobbsey Twins: